If I Were a Grown-up!

by Woody

The Millbrook Press
Brookfield, Connecticut

If I were a grown-up,
I would like to be
a doctor...

for aliens!

If I were a grown-up,
I would like to be
a painter...

of monkeys!

If I were a grown-up,
I would like to be
a farmer...

of ice cream!

If I were a grown-up,
I would like to be a
dentist...

for lions!

If I were a grown-up, I would like to be a ballet dancer...

under water!

If I were a grown-up,
I would like to be a vet...

for monsters!

Or maybe not!

What would you like to be?
doctor
painter
farmer